LUCY DOVE

by **Janice Del Negro**

illustrated by **Leonid Gore**

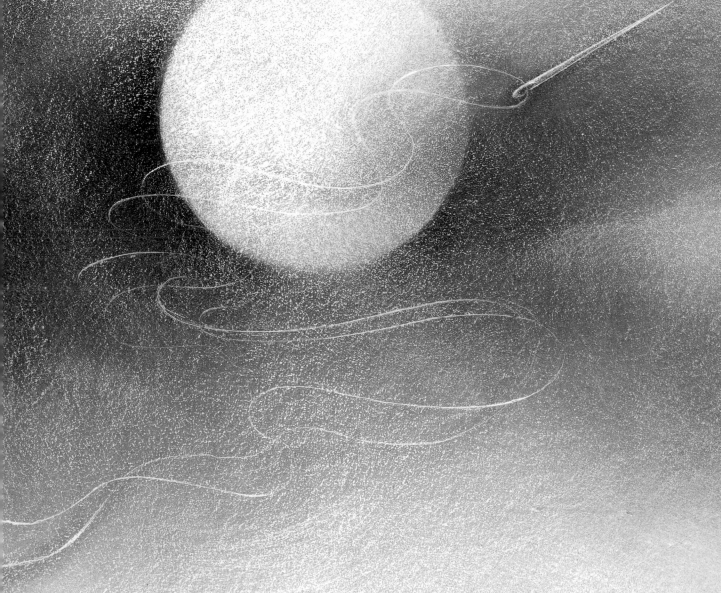

A DK INK BOOK

DK PUBLISHING, INC.

When wishes were horses and beggars could ride, in a stone castle by the sea there lived a rich laird. He was a good laird, as lairds go, with one great fault. He was superstitious. He believed in things like black cats being bad luck and four-leaf clovers being good. This laird had a soothsayer, a fortune-teller, who one day told the laird that if he could get a pair of trousers sewn by the light of the full moon in the graveyard of old St. Andrew's church, the trousers would bring him good fortune.

Now, there were stories about St. Andrew's, and everybody knew them—stories that said the abandoned churchyard was haunted by some fearsome thing. There had been many brave and foolish men who, upon hearing the tales about the churchyard, went in the night to find out what was happening there. And what they found they'll never tell, for none of them was ever seen again. So there was good reason why no one ever went there after dark, full moon or no. But that didn't stop the laird.

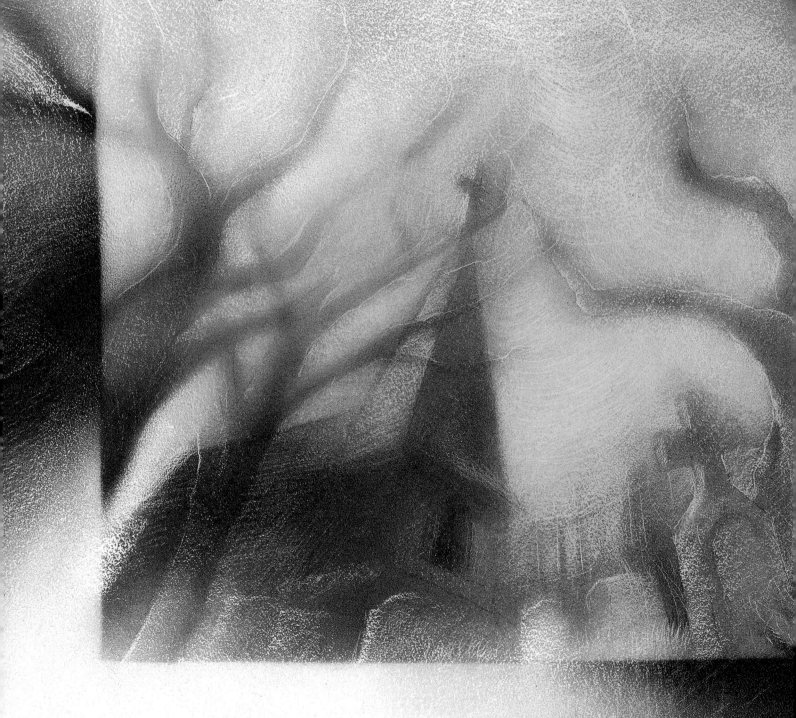

"Write a proclamation!" he bellowed. "A sackful of gold to the one who sews me those trews!" He let it be known that he expected the trousers the following Saturday—the first night of the next full moon, thank you very much—or else he'd know the reason why.

As fortune would have it, and fortune always has her way, Lucy Dove heard about the laird and his need for lucky trousers. A seamstress by profession, Lucy Dove could use that sackful of gold, having recently been sacked from the laird's own household. Oh, she still had a clever needle, but her sewing had slowed with age, and not even a soothsayer could foresee sacks of gold in her future. Reading the proclamation, Lucy saw her way clear to a comfortable old age, in a cottage of her own, on her own piece of shore.

"Well, I'm old enough to know a thing or two about churchyards, and soothsayers, and foolish lairds, too. If it's trousers sewn by the light of the moon he wants, it's trousers sewn by the light of the moon he'll get, and a dear sum he'll pay for them, moonluck and all!"

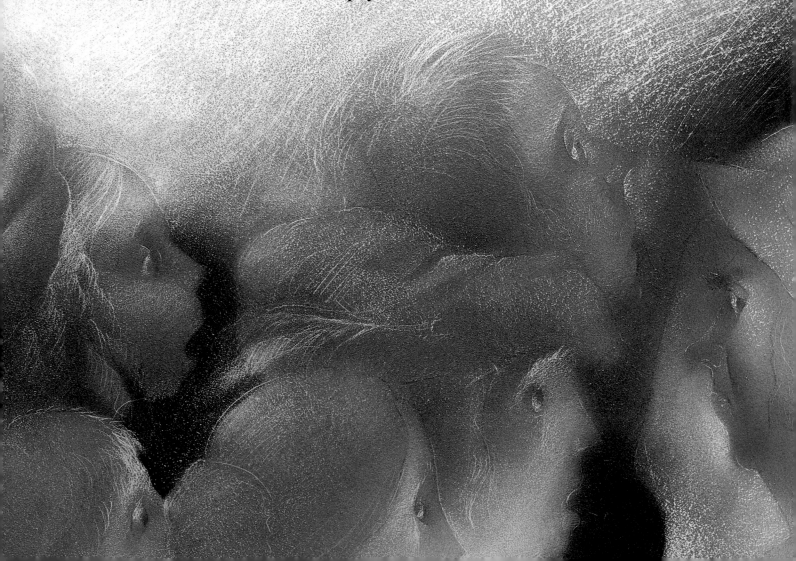

With just enough money not to freeze or go hungry, Lucy Dove pulled out her scrap bag and waited for Saturday. When it came, she pinned and basted motley scraps into trousers to fit the laird, threaded her needles, and set out her shears. In the twilight space between sunset and moonrise, she gathered scraps, needles, shears, and all into her apron and set out for old St. Andrew's.

The moon was rising full when Lucy stood before the church. Abandoned when the stories began, it was dark and empty, the churchyard long neglected.

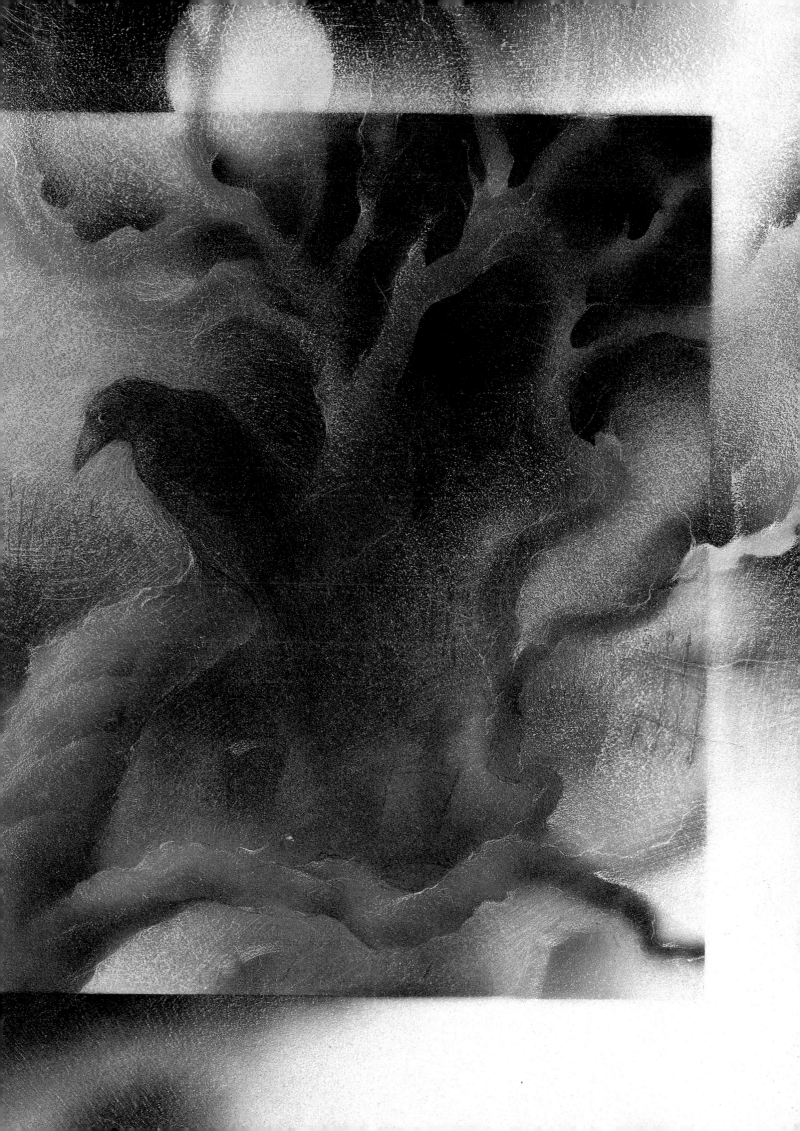

Lucy chose to sit where the moon shone its brightest, on a flat gravestone next to a marble tomb.

She shook out the pinned and basted cloth, then licked her thread and began to sew. And sew . . . and sew . . . each stitch even and straight.

Just as she was beginning to think the stories she'd heard about the churchyard were just that, stories, a strange, unpleasant smell filled the air. It was the smell of dampness and decay. It was the smell of graves and corruption. It was the smell of death, without the promise of eternity to redeem it.

Lucy kept sewing, and the smell grew stronger, and stronger still, until there was a tremendous crash and the marble tomb beside her split in two.

From amidst the broken stone emerged a monstrous, misshapen head, sunken eyes burning with the devil's own fire. It spoke. "Do you see this great head of mine? Long have I lacked blood and meat, so now it is just skin and bone, bone and marrow, skin and bone, bone and marrow."

Lucy's throat was dry as dust, but fixing her heart on a hearth of her own and a sackful of gold, she managed to reply pleasantly enough. "Hmmm? Have you been here all along? I'm so sorry, I didn't notice." Her hands never stopped moving as on she sewed, each stitch even and straight.

From beneath the dark earth the fearsome thing rose higher, its ropy neck twisted and thick.

"Do you see this twisted neck of mine, old woman? Long have I lacked blood and meat, so now it is just skin and bone, bone and marrow, skin and bone, bone and marrow."

"Skin and bone, bone and . . . ? Oh, I know. You're the wee bogle they tell those stories about." Lucy's hands barely shook as on she sewed, each stitch even and straight.

"Stories? About me?" The bogle drew one great, twisted arm out of the tomb's rubble and leaned upon it. "Do they tell of my fearsome visage? Of how I strike fear in the hearts of brave but foolish men?"

"Something like that." Lucy, her hands ever moving, looked the gruesome thing up and down and gave a little sniff. "They tell them to little children at bedtime, to help them sleep, you know."

"Little children?" the monster snarled. "Bedtime stories? Look here, old woman."

Lucy looked. From under the earth came the second long, twisted arm, an arm that ended not in a long, twisted hand like the other, but in five jagged claws that slashed the air and clutched for Lucy Dove, but could not reach her.

"Old woman, do you see these great arms of mine? Long have I lacked blood and meat, so now they are just skin and bone, bone and marrow."

"Oh, I see them," said Lucy. "Really, it's amazing how some people exaggerate for the sake of a good story." Her hands flew, and though her stitches got a bit longer, they were as neat as ever.

The writhing creature strained and stretched, taller and taller. It loomed over Lucy Dove, and with a terrifying hiss pulled one great, twisted leg out of the grave and stamped it on the ground.

Grinning a horrible grin, the hideous thing leaned closer, showing sharp, pointed teeth, exhaling a malodorous cloud around Lucy Dove. "Old woman, do you see this great leg of mine? Long have I lacked blood and meat, so now it is just skin and bone, bone and marrow, skin and bone—"

"Be hard not to see it, and smell it," Lucy snapped, thinking of how she'd like to have missed it entirely. "No need to get unpleasant."

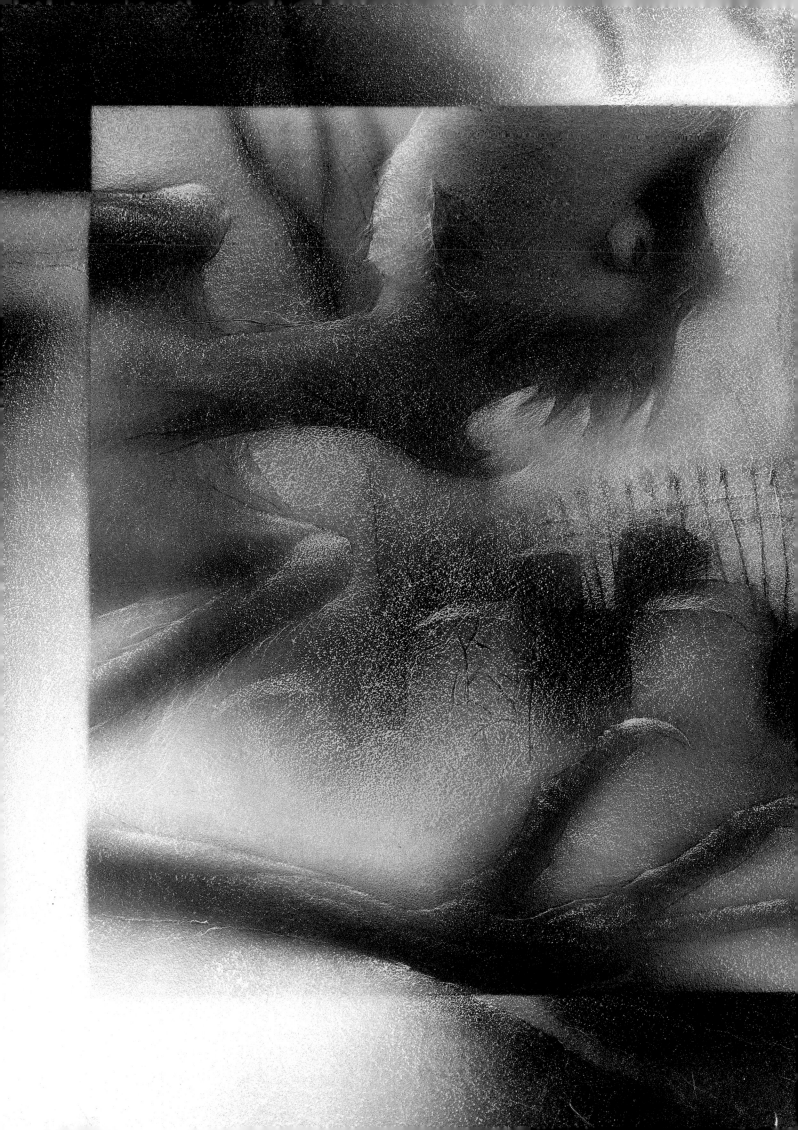

Holding her breath, Lucy stitched her last stitch, knotted her thread, and leaped to her feet. Lucky trousers in hand, her old limbs given youth by the promise of success, she ran through the churchyard gate.

The monster stared, confounded, giving Lucy a precious few steps. Then, "Stop, old woman, stop! No one gets away from me!" The fearsome bogle yanked its second leg from beneath the earth and with angry strides gave chase after Lucy Dove.

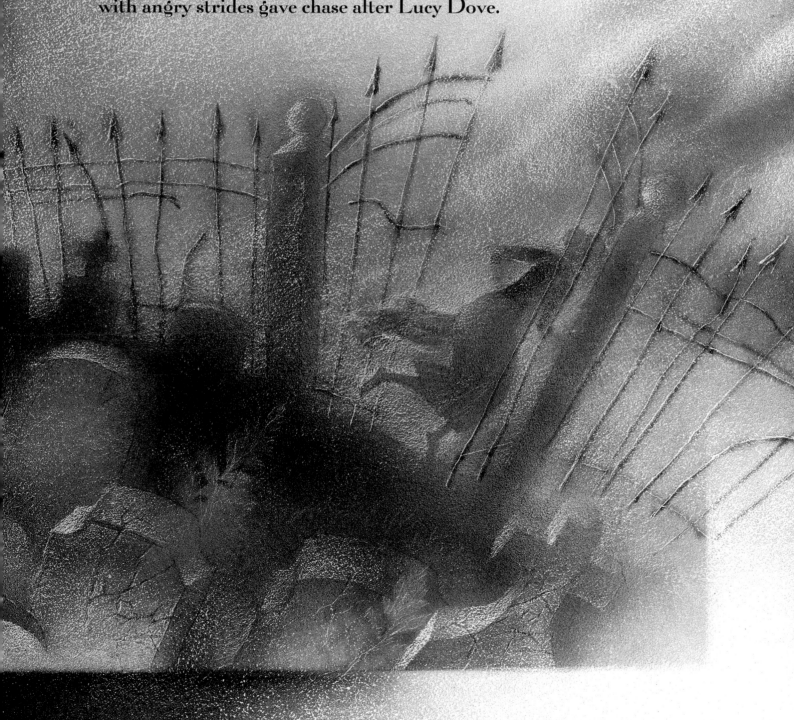

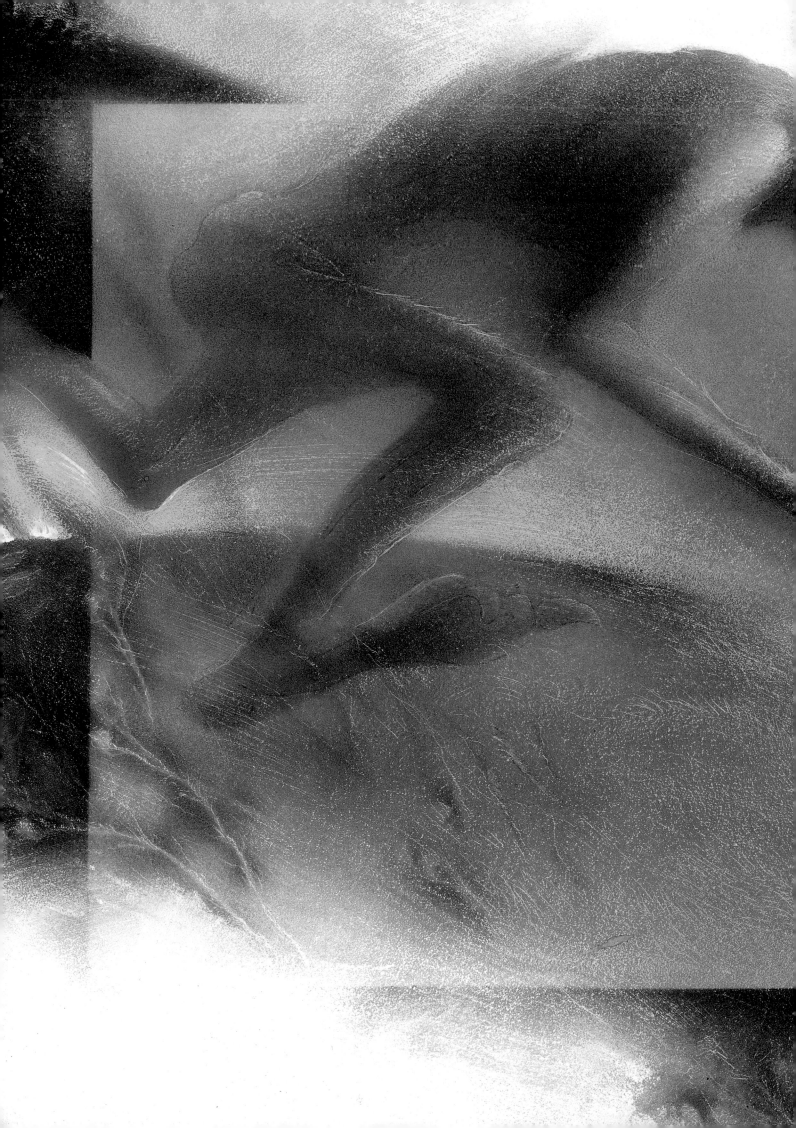

Down the hill they raced, the monster ever gaining, but Lucy had a good head start, and though the thing roared after her to stop, she never looked behind her. She set her mind on her own piece of shore, clutched those lucky trousers to her chest, and ran.

She ran until she reached the gate of the laird's castle by the sea, a wooden gate, a strong gate, a locked gate—a gate bolted shut against the night and all the things that roam it. Lucy Dove pounded on the gate —pounded, she had no breath to call for help. She looked back then, only to see the long, jagged claws slash through the air, reaching for her, reaching . . .

   . . . when the castle gate opened just a crack, and Lucy slipped inside.

   The bogle let loose a wail that shook the sky, and in a starving rage it raked the arch above the gate with those foul claws, leaving five deep grooves in the hard, cold stone.

That is how the laird got his lucky trousers, and how Lucy Dove gained a bag of gold. And if it was trousers full of moonluck that helped her beat a bogle in a race, who's to say yea or no? As for that fearsome creature, it was not seen again, although it left its mark for all to see. Five claw marks in hard stone—made as easily as the lines Lucy Dove made in the sand, in front of her own cottage, on her own piece of shore.

For Miranda and Willa
J. D. N.

To my aunts
L. G.

"Lucy Dove" is an original character and tale based on traditional sources and variants, primarily "The Sprightly Tailor" in Joseph Jacobs's *Celtic Fairy Tales* (G.P. Putnam & Sons, 1892) and "The Grey Claw" in Winifred Finlay's *Tales of Fantasy and Fear* (Kaye and Ward, 1981). There is also a single-tale version by Paul Galdone called *The Monster and the Tailor* (Clarion, 1982).

A Melanie Kroupa Book

DK Publishing, Inc., 95 Madison Avenue, New York, New York 10016

Visit us on the World Wide Web at http://www.dk.com

Library of Congress Cataloging-in-Publication Data
Del Negro, Janice
Lucy Dove / by Janice Del Negro ; illustrations by Leonid Gore. — 1st ed.
    p.   cm.
    Summary: While sewing the laird's trews by moonlight in a haunted churchyard in return for a sackful of gold, an aging seamstress outwits a terrible monster.
    ISBN 0-7894-2511-9
    [1. Monsters—Fiction. 2. Scotland—Fiction.] I. Gore, Leonid, ill. II. Title.
    PZ7.D3853Lu 1998   97-43607
    [E]—dc21   CIP
                                                            AC

Book design by Leonid Gore and Chris Hammill Paul. The text of this book is set in 17 point Belucian.
The illustrations for this book were painted in acrylics.

Stoddart
Kids

Published in Canada in 1998 by Stoddart Kids, a division of Stoddart Publishing Co. Limited, 34 Lesmill Road, Toronto, Canada M3B 2T6
Distributed in Canada by General Distribution Services, 30 Lesmill Road, Toronto, Canada M3B 2T6
Tel (416) 445-3333   Fax (416) 445-5967   E-mail Customer.Service@ccmailgw.genpub.com

Canadian Cataloguing in Publication Data
Del Negro, Janice Lucy Dove
ISBN 0-7737-3107-5 I. Gore, Leonid. II. Title.
PZ7.D486Lu 1998   j813.54   C98-930696-8

Printed and bound in the U.S.A.
First Edition, 1998
2 4 6 8 10 9 7 5 3 1